BONE SOUP

by

CAMBRIA
EVANS

Houghton Mifflin Company

BOSTON 2008

R.I.P.

DEDICATED to

KARI

IN MEMORIAM
M.S. "PIGGERS" PIG

special thanks
to
judy-sue
the studio
+
kate o'sullivan
cara llewellyn

All rights reserved. For information about permission to reproduce selections from this book, write to Permissions, Houghton Mifflin Company, 215 Park Avenue South, New York, New York 10003.

www.houghtonmifflinbooks.com

The text of this book is set in Broadsheet.
The illustrations are pen, watercolor, and collage with digital color.

Library of Congress Cataloging-in-Publication data is on file.
ISBN-13: 978-0-618-80908-0

Printed in Singapore
TWP 10 9 8 7 6 5 4 3 2 1

Being nothing more than skin and bone, Finnigin had to live by his wits. He had no family or house to haunt, but he was known across the land for having a ravenous appetite. Everyone knew that wherever Finnigin went, he always brought his eating stool, his eating spoon, and his gigantic eating mouth.

EATING STOOL

EATING SPOON

EATING MOUTH

One Halloween, Finnigin's travels took him through a barren land. *What a lovely place,* he thought. *I'm sure I can find a Halloween feast here.* But as Finnigin grew closer to town, a witch passed by.

"Happy Hallows Night," he said. "Do you know where the feast is?" The witch took one look at Finnigin and quickly flew away.

Back in town, the witch told the beast, the beast told the zombies, the zombies told the mummy, and before you knew it, the entire town was talking about the impending arrival of Finnigin the Eater.

In a panic, the witch booby-trapped her jars of eyeballs,

the beast locked his bat wings in a cupboard,

the zombies put their frog legs in the cellar,

and the mummy and other towns-creatures hid all they had to eat.

When poor, ever-hungry Finnigin came to town, he was surprised that it looked empty, but even more surprised that there was no feast.

So, Finnigin knocked on the witch's door first. "Could you spare a bit of food?" he called out. "I have nothing for *you*!" the witch shrieked.

Next Finnigin tried the beast's door. "Could you spare some wormy cheese and bread for a simple traveler?" he asked.

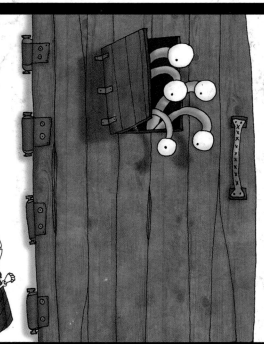

"A simple traveler?" the beast said. "I know who you are! I have just enough for myself, and none to spare. Be gone!"

At the third door Finnigin had barely opened his mouth when the zombies all yelled, "Go away! We've no food for you!" At the mummy's door the answer was the same.

And so he went through the whole town, knocking on doors and windows. But not a body or soul had any food for Finnigin.

Undaunted, Finnigin collected wood from the forest and built a fire in the middle of the town square. He then filled the town's largest cauldron with water and set it to boil.

After waiting a time, Finnigin ceremoniously opened his cloak. He took out a magnificent piece of bone, so old that the edges were dry and splintered, and with a toothy grin, he dropped it right into the cauldron.

Finnigin stirred the mixture, singing,

One by one, the townscreatures opened their doors and walked toward Finnigin and his fire.

Finnigin smiled. "Well, then I must not be a ghoul, for I am making such a soup."

The little werewolf crouched at Finnigin's side. "I've never heard of bone soup before, but I think I'll like it."

"In some places I have traveled, bone soup is considered a delicacy," Finnigin explained. "Besides, this is no ordinary bone. It is magic."

He tasted the broth again and sighed. "If only there were some stewed eyeballs. With eyeballs, the soup would be very tasty."

The little werewolf tugged at Finnigin's cloak.
"The witch has jars of those—I know she does."

All the villagers stared at the witch, and her face turned an even brighter shade of green. "Y—yes, I do," she stammered, "but they're imported . . ."

The villagers stared at the witch until she finally fetched some from her stash.

The eyeballs were a fabulous addition to the soup, but soon Finnigin looked wistful.

"If only this had some bat wings. Can you just imagine what flavor they would add?"

The little werewolf tugged at Finnigin again. "The beast has cupboards full of those. I saw them myself."

Embarrassed, the beast fetched an entire box of bat wings. The wings were added, and just as Finnigin had said, their flavor was wonderful.

Finnigin continued to stir the soup, but he looked longingly into the cauldron.

"Now, if only we had frog legs, this soup would be fit for a king!"

The little werewolf tugged once more on Finnigin's cloak. "The zombies have a cellar filled with those—just ask them." Before Finnigin could ask, the zombie children had fetched all the frog legs they could carry.

The frog legs were stirred into the broth, and soon the cauldron was also bubbling with

SPIDER EGGS,

DRIED MOUSE DROPPINGS,

TOENAIL CLIPPINGS,

AND DANDELIONS.

With a final dusting of slime and sludge, the soup was declared ready.

"Of course, this soup is wonderful alone," said Finnigin, "but it takes only wormy cheese, bread, and company to make it a true Halloween feast. Go, bring your cheese, bread, and bowls so we can share this bone soup together!"

WHAT A **FABULOUS** SOUP!

SUCH GOOD **FLAVOR!**

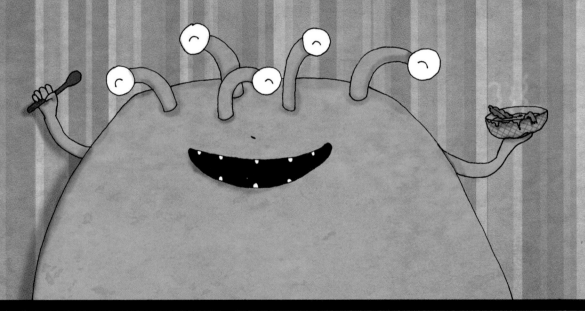

TRULY FIT FOR A KING!

TO THINK, IT WAS ALL MADE FROM A **MAGIC BONE!**

And so it was that Finnigin got his Halloween feast after all.

With a final wave to the werewolf, Finnigin quickly left with his eating stool, his eating spoon, and his gigantic smiling mouth.